The Enchanted Horse

and other magical stories

Compiled by Vic Parker

Miles Kelly

First published in 2012 by Miles Kelly Publishing Ltd
Harding's Barn, Bardfield End Green, Thaxted, Essex, CM6 3PX, UK

2 4 6 8 10 9 7 5 3 1

Publishing Director Belinda Gallagher
Creative Director Jo Cowan
Editorial Director Rosie McGuire
Editor Carly Blake
Senior Designer Joe Jones
Editorial Assistant Lauren White
Production Manager Elizabeth Collins
Reprographics Anthony Cambray, Stephan Davis, Jennifer Hunt

ISBN 978-1-84810-577-5

Printed in China

British Library Cataloguing-in-Publication Data
A catalogue record for this book is available from the British Library

ACKNOWLEDGEMENTS

The publishers would like to thank the following artists who have contributed to this book:
Advocate Art: Alida Massari
The Bright Agency: Marcin Piwowarski (inc. cover), Tom Sperling
Marsela Hajdinjak
All other artwork from the Miles Kelly Artwork Bank

The publishers would like to thank the following sources for the use of their photographs:
Shutterstock: (page decorations) Dragana Francuski Tolimir
Dreamstime: (frames) Gordan

Every effort has been made to acknowledge the source and copyright holder of each picture.
Miles Kelly Publishing apologises for any unintentional errors or omissions.

Made with paper from a sustainable forest

www.mileskelly.net   info@mileskelly.net

www.factsforprojects.com

Contents

The Enchanted Horse

From *The Arabian Nights Entertainments*,
adapted by Amy Steedman

IT WAS NEW YEAR'S day in Persia, and the king had been entertained by many wonderful shows prepared for him by his people. Evening was drawing in when an Indian appeared, leading a horse he wished to show to the king. It was not real, but it was so wonderfully made that it looked alive.

"Your Majesty," cried the Indian, bowing low, "I beg thou wilt look upon this wonder. Nothing thou hast seen today can equal my horse. I have only to mount upon its back and wish myself in any part of the world, and it carries me there in a few minutes."

"Show us what it can do," the king commanded.

He pointed to a distant mountain, and bade the Indian to fetch a branch from the palm trees there.

The Indian vaulted into the saddle, turned a little peg in the horse's neck, and in a moment was flying so swiftly through the air that he soon disappeared from sight. In less than a quarter of an hour he reappeared, and laid a branch from a palm tree at the king's feet.

"Thou art right," cried the king. "Thy enchanted horse is the most wonderful thing I have seen. What is its price? I must have it!"

"Your Majesty," the Indian replied, "it shall be thine only if thou wilt give me your daughter, for my wife."

At these words the king's son sprang to his feet.

"Sire," he cried, "thou wilt never dream of granting such a request."

"My son," answered the king, "at whatever cost I must have this wonderful horse. But before I agree, try the horse, and tell me what thou thinkest of it."

The Indian began to tell the prince how to work the horse. But as soon as the prince was in the saddle, he turned the screw and went flying off through the air.

"Alas!" cried the Indian, "he has gone off without learning how to come back!"

"Wretch," the king cried, "thou shalt be cast into prison, and unless my son returns in safety, thou shalt be put to death."

Meanwhile the prince had gone gaily sailing up into the clouds, and could no longer see the Earth below. This was very pleasant, and he felt that he had never had such a delicious ride in his life before. But presently he began to think it was time to descend. He screwed the peg round and round, backwards

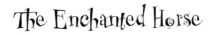

and forwards, but it seemed to make no difference.

Instead of coming down he sailed higher and higher, until he thought he was going to knock his head against the blue sky.

What was to be done? The prince began to grow a little nervous, and he felt over the horse's neck to see if there was another peg to be found anywhere. To his joy, just behind the ear, he touched a small screw, and when he turned it, he felt he was going slower and slower, and gently turning round. Then the Enchanted Horse flew downwards through the starry night, and he saw, stretched out before him, a beautiful city gleaming white through the purple night.

He let the horse go where it would, and presently it stopped on the roof of a great marble palace. He descended some white marble steps and found himself in a great hall where a row of slaves were sleeping soundly, guarding the entrance to a room beyond. Very softly the prince crept past the guards, and lifting the curtain from the door, looked in. And there he saw a splendid room lit by a thousand lights and filled with sleeping slaves, and in the middle, upon a sofa, was the most beautiful princess his eyes had ever gazed upon. He went softly to her side, and, kneeling by the sofa, gently touched her hand. The princess sighed and opened her eyes, but before she could cry out, he begged her in a whisper to be silent and fear nothing.

"I am a prince," he said, "the son of the King of Persia."

Now this princess was no other than the daughter of the King of Bengal.

Never before had the princess seen anyone so gallant and handsome as this strange young prince. She gave him her hand, awoke her slaves and bade them give him refreshment. While the prince rested, she dressed herself in her loveliest robes, and twined her hair with her most precious jewels, that she might appear as beautiful as possible. And when the prince saw her again, he thought her the most charming princess in all the world, and he loved her with all his heart. When he had told her all his adventures she sighed to think that he must now leave her and return to his father's court.

"My princess," he said, "since it is so hard to part, wilt thou not ride with me upon the Enchanted Horse? Then when we arrive once more in Persia we will marry."

So together they mounted the Enchanted Horse and the prince placed his arm around the princess and turned the magic peg. Up and up they flew over land and sea, and then the prince turned the other screw, and they landed just outside his father's city. He left the princess at a palace outside the gates, for he wished to go alone to prepare his father.

"My beloved son!" cried the king, full of joy at his safe return.

And the prince told the king all about his adventure and the Princess of Bengal.

"Let her be brought here instantly," cried the king, "and the marriage shall take place today." Then he ordered that the Indian should be set free at once and allowed to depart with the Enchanted Horse.

Great was the surprise of the Indian when he was released instead of having his head cut off, as he had expected. But when he heard about the prince's adventure, a wicked plan came into his head. He flew on the Enchanted Horse to the palace where the princess was waiting, arriving before the king's messengers could reach her. "Tell the princess," he said to the palace slaves, "that the Prince of Persia has sent me to bring her to his father's palace upon the Enchanted Horse."

The princess was very glad when she heard this message – but alas! As soon as the Indian turned the peg and the horse flew away, she found she was being carried off, far away from Persia and her beloved prince. All her prayers and entreaties were in vain. The Indian only mocked her and said he meant to marry her himself.

When the prince discovered what had happened, he was beside himself with grief. He set off to seek for her, vowing that he would find her, or perish in the attempt.

By this time the Enchanted Horse had travelled many hundreds of miles. The Indian descended into a wood close to the town of Cashmere, where he went in search of food. As soon as the princess had eaten a little she felt stronger and braver, and as she heard horses galloping past, she called out loudly for help. The men on horseback came riding at once to her aid. The leader of the horsemen, who was the Sultan of Cashmere, cut off the Indian's head, placed the princess upon his horse and led her to his palace. He had made up his mind to marry her himself!

In vain the princess begged and pleaded to be sent back to Persia. But the sultan only smiled and began the wedding preparations. Then she thought of a plan to save herself. She began talking all the nonsense she could think of and behaving as if she were mad. So well did she pretend, that the wedding was put off, and all the doctors were called in to see if they could cure her. Of course, none of them could.

All this time the Prince of Persia was searching for his princess, and when he came to one of the great cities of India, he quickly learned that everyone was talking about the sad illness of the Princess of Bengal who was to marry the sultan. He at once disguised himself as a doctor and went to the palace. The sultan received him with joy, and led him at once to where the princess sat alone, weeping and wringing her hands.

"Your Majesty," said the disguised prince, "no one must enter the room with me, or the cure will surely fail and the princess will never recover."

So the sultan left him, and the prince went to the princess, and gently touched her hand. "My beloved princess," he said, "dost thou not know me?"

As soon as the princess heard that dear voice she threw herself into the prince's arms.

"We must at once plan our escape," said the prince. "Canst thou tell me what has become of the Enchanted Horse?"

"Naught can I tell thee of it, dear prince," answered the princess, "but since the sultan knows its value, no doubt he has kept it in some safe place."

"Then first we must persuade the sultan that thou art almost cured," said the prince. "Put on thy costliest robes and dine with him tonight, and I will do the rest."

The sultan was charmed to find the princess so

much recovered, and his joy knew no bounds when the new doctor informed him that he hoped by the next day to have complete the cure.

"I find that the princess has somehow been infected by the magic of the Enchanted Horse," he said. "If thou wilt have the horse brought out into the great square, and place the princess upon its back, I will prepare some magic perfumes which will dispel the enchantment."

So next morning the Enchanted Horse was brought out into the square, which was crowded with onlookers, and the princess was mounted upon its back. Then the disguised prince placed four braziers of burning coals round the horse and threw into them a perfume of a most delicious scent. The smoke of the perfume rose in thick clouds, almost hiding the princess, and at that moment the prince leaped into the saddle behind her, turned the peg, and sailed away into the blue sky.

The Enchanted Horse did not stop until it had

carried the two of them safely back to Persia, and there they were married amid great rejoicings.

But what became of the Enchanted Horse? Ah! That is a question which no one can answer.

The Princess on the Glass Hill

From Andrew Lang's *Blue Fairy Book*

ONCE UPON A TIME there was a man who had a meadow which lay on a mountain, and in the meadow there was a barn in which he stored hay. But there had not been much hay for the last two years, for every St John's eve, when the grass was highest, it was all eaten clean up, as if a whole flock of sheep had gnawed it during the night. The man became tired of losing his crop, and said to his sons – he had three of them, and the third was called Cinderlad – that one of them must sleep in the barn on St John's night and keep a sharp look-out, to stop whatever was destroying the grass.

The eldest was quite willing to go to the meadow. He would watch so well, he said, that neither man, nor beast, nor even the Devil himself should have any of it. So when evening came he went to the barn and lay down to sleep, but when night was drawing on there was such a rumbling and earthquake that the walls and roof shook. The lad took to his heels as fast as he could, never even looking back, so the barn remained empty that year too.

Next St John's eve, the next oldest son was willing to show what he could do. He went to the barn and lay down to sleep, as his brother had done, but when night was drawing near there was a great rumbling, and then an earthquake even worse than that on the former St John's night. When the youth heard it he was terrified and went running off.

The year after, it was Cinderlad's turn, but when he made ready to go the others mocked him. "Well, you are just the right one to watch the hay, you who have never learned anything but how to sit among the ashes!" said they.

Cinderlad, however, did not trouble himself about what they said, but when evening drew near he rambled away to the outlying field. When he got there he went into the barn and lay down, but in about an hour's time the rumbling and creaking began, and it was frightful to hear it. 'Well, if it gets no worse than that, I can manage to stand it,' thought Cinderlad. In a little time the creaking began again, and the earth quaked so that all the hay flew about. 'Oh! If it gets no worse than that I can manage to stand it,' thought Cinderlad. But then came a third rumbling, and a third earthquake, so violent that the boy thought the walls and roof had fallen down, but when that was over everything suddenly grew as still. 'I am pretty sure that it will come again,' thought Cinderlad, but no, it did not. Everything was quiet, and everything stayed quiet, and when he had lain still a short time he heard

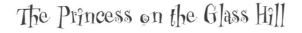

something that sounded as if a horse were standing chewing just outside the barn door.

He stole away to the door, which was ajar, to see what was there, and a horse was standing eating. It was so big, and fat, and fine a horse that Cinderlad had never seen one like it before, and a saddle and bridle lay upon it, and a complete suit of armour for a knight, and everything was of copper, and so bright that it shone. 'Ha, ha! It is thou who eatest up our hay then,' thought the boy. 'I will stop that'.

So he made haste, and took out his steel for striking fire, and threw it over the horse, and then it had no power to stir from the spot, and became so tame that the boy could do what he liked with it. So he mounted it and rode away to a place which no one knew of but himself, and there he tied it up.

When he went home again his brothers sniggered and asked how he had got on.

"I lay in the barn till the sun rose, but I saw nothing and heard nothing, not I," said the boy. "God knows what there was to make you two so frightened."

And when the puzzled brothers went to check the meadow, the grass was all standing just as long and as thick as it had been the night before.

The next St John's eve, Cinderlad went again, and three earthquakes happened exactly as before. This time the horse that arrived was far larger and fatter than the first horse, and it had a saddle on its back, and a bridle was on it too, and a full suit of armour for a knight, all of bright silver, and as beautiful as anyone could wish to see. Again the boy took out his steel for striking fire, and threw it over the horse's mane, and the beast stood there as quiet as a lamb. Then the boy rode the horse away to where he kept the other, and then went home again.

Once more, in the morning, the astounded brothers found the meadow grass standing as high and as thick as ever, but that did not make them any kinder to Cinderlad.

When the third St John's night came, once more Cinderlad dared to go, and everything happened just the same. There were three earthquakes, each worse than the last, and then there was a horse standing outside the barn, much larger and fatter than the two others he had caught. Again the boy pulled out his steel for striking fire, and threw it over the horse, and the boy could do just what he liked with it. He mounted it and rode to the place where he had the two others, and then he went home again.

21

The brothers hated him, for again the grass was standing, looking as fine and as thick as ever.

Now, the king of the country in which Cinderlad's father dwelled lived in a palace close to a high, high hill of glass, slippery as ice. One day, the king sent out a proclamation saying that he would give his daughter's hand in marriage – and half the kingdom – to any man who could ride up to the top of the glass hill, to where his daughter was to sit, and take one of three gold apples she would hold in her lap. On the appointed day, princes and knights came riding thither from the very end of the world to win the beautiful princess, and everyone else thronged to the glass hill to see who won her. Cinderlad's two brothers went along too, but they would not hear of letting him go with them, for he was so dirty with sleeping among the ashes that they said everyone would laugh at them if they were seen in the company of such an oaf.

"Well, then, I will go all alone by myself," said Cinderlad.

When the two brothers got to the glass hill, all the princes and knights were trying to ride up it – but in vain, for no sooner did the horses set foot upon the hill then down they slipped, and there was not one which could get even so much as a couple of yards up.

At last all the horses were so tired that they could do no more, and their riders were forced to give up the attempt.

When suddenly a knight in copper armour came riding up on a horse with copper bridle and saddle, shining like the dawn. He rode straight to the hill and began going up as if it were nothing at all. The princess thought that she had never seen so handsome a knight, and hoped that he might make it to the top. But when the knight had got about a third of the way up, he suddenly turned his horse round and rode down again. The disappointed princess threw one of the golden apples down after him, and it rolled into his shoe. But when he had come down from off the hill he rode away so fast that no one knew what had become of him.

That night, Cinderlad's brothers returned home with a long story to tell about the copper knight and his horse riding up the glass hill.

"Oh! I should have liked to see him too, that I should," said Cinderlad, who was as usual sitting by the chimney among the cinders.

Next day the brothers set out again, and once

more refused to let Cinderlad go with them.

All the princes and knights were beginning to ride again, and this time they had taken care to roughen the shoes of their horses – but that did not help them. They rode and they slipped as they had done the day before, and not one of them could get even so far as a yard up the hill. When they had tired out their horses, they again had to stop altogether.

But all at once a knight in silver armour came riding on a steed that was much, much finer than the horse in copper tack. This one had a silver bridle and saddle, and he and his rider shone like the moon. He rode straight to the glass hill and began to go up. The princess liked this knight even better than she had liked the other, and sat longing that he might be able to get all the way up. But when the knight had ridden two-thirds of the way up he suddenly turned his horse around and rode down again. The dismayed princess threw an apple after him, and it rolled into his shoe, and as soon as he had got down the glass hill he rode away so fast that no one could see what had become of him.

At night the two brothers went home full of news of the knight in silver armour.

"Oh, how I should have liked to see him too!" said Cinderlad, from the dirt of the woodpile.

On the third day everything went just as on the former days. Cinderlad wanted to go with them to look at the riding, but the two brothers would not have him, and when they got to the glass hill there was no one who could ride even so far as a yard up it. Then there came thundering a knight in golden armour, riding a stallion without equal, wearing a golden saddle and bridle, and they blazed like the noonday sun. The knight rode straight away to the glass hill, and galloped up it as if it were no hill at all, so that the princess had not even time to wish that he might get up the whole way before he was at the top. The golden knight took the third golden apple from the lap of the princess and then turned his horse about and rode down again, and vanished from their sight before anyone was able to say a word to him.

When the two brothers returned home again, they told Cinderlad all about the knight in the golden armour.

"Oh, if only I could have seen him!" said Cinderlad, scrubbing the scullery floor.

Next day all the knights and princes were to appear before the king and princess, in order that he who had the golden apple might produce it. One after the other they all came, but no one had the golden apple. First princes, then knights went… then all the other young men of the kingdom. Cinderlad's two brothers were the last of all, and the king enquired of them if there was no one else left to come.

"We have a brother," said the two, "but he never got the golden apple! He never left the kitchen on any of the three days."

"Never mind that," said the king. "As everyone else has come to the palace, let him come too."

So Cinderlad was made to go to the king's palace.

"Hast thou the golden apple?" asked the king.

"Yes, here is the first, and here is the second, and here is the third, too," said Cinderlad, and he took all three apples out of his pocket, and with that drew off his sooty rags, and appeared there before them in his bright golden armour, which gleamed as he stood.

"Thou shalt have my daughter, and the half of my kingdom, and thou hast well earned both!" said the king. So there was a wedding, and Cinderlad got the king's daughter, and everyone made merry at the wedding, for all of them could make merry, even though they could not ride up the glass hill. And if they have not left off their merry-making they must be at it still.

The Star and the Lily

From *Indian Myths*
by Ellen Russell Emerson

AN OLD CHIEFTAIN was sitting in his wigwam, quietly smoking his favourite pipe, when a crowd of Indian boys and girls suddenly entered and begged him to tell them all a story, and he did so.

There was once a time when this world was filled with happy people, when all the nations were as one, and the crimson tide of war had not begun to roll. Plenty of game was in the forest and on the plains. Every tree and bush yielded fruit. Flowers carpeted the earth. Birds flew from branch to

branch, fearing none, for there were none to harm
them. The beasts of the field were tame, and they
came and went at the bidding of man. One long
unending spring gave no place for winter, and
sickness was unknown.

It was at such a time, when Earth was a paradise
and humans worthy to be in charge, that the Indians
were the only dwellers in the American wilderness.
They numbered millions, and, living as nature
designed them to live, enjoyed its many blessings.
At night they met on the wide green beneath the
heavenly worlds. They watched the stars – they
loved to gaze at them, for they believed them to be
the homes of the good, who had been taken home
by the Great Spirit.

One night they saw one star brighter than all
others. It was far away in the south, near a mountain
peak. For many nights it was seen, till at length
many began to doubt that the star was as far distant
as it seemed to be. People began to think it must be

only a short distance away, near the tops of some trees. A number of warriors went to see what it was, and on their return said it appeared strange and somewhat like a bird. A committee of wise men feared that it might be the omen of some disaster – perhaps the star spoken of by their forefathers as the forerunner of a dreadful war. However, others thought it foretold good.

One moon had nearly gone by, and yet the mystery remained unsolved. One night a young warrior had a dream, in which a beautiful maiden came and stood at his side. She told him, "Young brave! Charmed with the land of my forefathers, its flowers, its birds, its rivers, its beautiful lakes, and its mountains, I have left my sisters in yonder world to dwell among you. Young brave! Ask your wise and your great men where I can live and see the happy race continually. Ask them what form I shall assume in order to be loved."

When the young man awoke, he assembled the

wise men of the nation and related his dream. They concluded that the star that had been seen in the south had fallen in love with mankind and that it wanted to live with them.

The next night, five tall, noble-looking and adventurous braves were sent to welcome the stranger to Earth. They went and presented to it a pipe of peace, filled with sweet-scented herbs, and were rejoiced that it took it from them. As they returned to the village, the star, with expanded wings, followed, and hovered over their homes till the dawn of day.

Again it came to the young man in a dream and desired to know where it should live and what form it should take. Places were named – on the top of giant trees, or in flowers. At length it was told to choose a place itself. At first it dwelled in the white

rose of the mountains,
but there it could not be seen. It went next to
the prairie, but it feared the hoof of the buffalo.
It then sought the rocky cliff, but there it was so
high that the children, whom it loved most out of
everything, could not see it.

"I know where I shall live," said the bright
fugitive, "where I can see the gliding canoe of
the race I most admire. Children! Yes, they shall be
my playmates. I will kiss their slumber by the side of
cool lakes. The nation shall love me wherever I am."

These words having been said, she alighted on the
waters, where she saw herself reflected.
And the next morning thousands of white
flowers were seen on the surface of the lakes.

This star lived in the
southern skies. Her brethren

can be seen far off in the cold north, hunting the Great Bear, whilst her sisters watch her in the east and west.

Children! When you see the lily on the waters, take it in your hands and hold it to the skies, that it may be happy on Earth, as its two sisters, the morning and evening stars, are happy in heaven.

The Well of the World's End

From *English Fairy Tales* by Joseph Jacobs

ONCE UPON A TIME there was a girl whose mother had died, and her father married again. And her stepmother hated her because she was more beautiful than herself. She used to make her do all the work, and never let her have any peace. One day, the stepmother thought to get rid of her altogether, so she handed her a sieve and said: "Go, fill it at the Well of the World's End and bring it home to me full, or woe betide you." For the stepmother thought the girl would never be able to find the Well of the World's End, and, if she did, how could she bring home a sieve full of water?

Well, the girl started off, and asked everyone she met where the Well of the World's End was. But nobody knew, and she didn't know what to do, when a little old woman, all bent double, told her how to get to it. So at last she arrived there, but when she dipped the sieve in the cold, cold water, it all ran out again. She tried and tried, but every time it was the same, and at last she sat down and cried as if her heart would break.

Suddenly she heard a croak, and she looked up and saw a great frog with goggle eyes looking at her.

"What's the matter, dearie?" it said.

The girl explained, and the frog replied: "If you promise me to do whatever I bid you for a whole night long, I'll tell you how to fill the sieve."

The girl didn't like the idea, but she had no choice, so she agreed. And the frog said:

Stop it with moss and daub it with clay,
And then it will carry the water away.

Then it gave a hop, skip, and jump, and jumped –
flop – back into the Well of the World's End.

So the girl lined the sieve with moss, and over
that she put some clay, and then she dipped it once
again into the Well of the World's End, and this time,
the water didn't run out.

Quite forgetting her promise to the frog, she
went back to her stepmother, who was angry as
angry, but said nothing at all.

That very evening they heard something tap-
tapping at the door low down, and a voice cried out:
"Open the door, my darling!"

The girl went and opened the door and, to her
dismay, there was the frog from the Well of the
World's End. She explained about the agreement,
and her stepmother said: "Girls must keep their
promises!" For she was quite gleeful that the girl
would have to obey a nasty frog.

And it hopped, and it hopped, and it jumped, till
it was right inside and then it said: "Let me sit on

your knee, my dear!"

But the girl didn't like to, till her stepmother said: "Lift it up this instant! Girls must keep their promises!"

So at last she lifted the frog up on to her lap, and it lay there for a time, till at last it said: "Give me some supper, my sweetheart!"

Well, she didn't mind doing that, so she got it a bowl of milk and bread, and fed it well. And when the frog had finished, it said: "Now, go with me to bed, my own one!"

But that the girl wouldn't do, till her stepmother said: "Do what you promised, or out you go, you and your froggie."

So the girl took the frog with her to bed, and kept it as far away from her as she could. Well, just as the day was beginning to break what should the frog say but: "Chop off my head, my true love. Remember the promise you made to me!"

At first the girl wouldn't, for she thought of what

the frog had done for her at the Well of the World's End. But when the frog said the words over again, she took an axe up and chopped off its head.

Lo and behold! There stood before her a handsome young prince, who told her that he had been enchanted by a wicked magician, and he could never be unspelled till some girl would do his bidding for a whole night, and chop off his head at the end of it.

So the prince and the girl were married and went away to live in the castle of the king, his father, and the stepmother hated every bit of it!